Barbie™

Girls on Blades

Written by Mona Miller

Photography by Lee Katz, Shirley Ushirogata, Greg Roccia, Mark Adams, and Jack Keely

g A GOLDEN BOOK · NEW YORK

Golden Books Publishing Company, Inc., New York, New York 10106

"I'll get there first!"

"No you won't! I'm going to beat you today!"

Amy and Diane raced on their skates toward the big oak tree in the park. They skidded to a stop in front of it at the exact same moment.

"TIE!" both girls yelled. They threw their arms around each other and laughed.

Every afternoon after school, Amy and Diane met Coach Barbie under the tree for in-line skating practice. Only today, something was different. . . .

"Where's Barbie?" Diane asked. "She's usually here first."

"Hello, girls," Barbie said, skating up behind them. "Sorry I'm late, but I stopped to picked this up."

"What is it?" both girls asked. They had noticed Barbie was holding a flyer.

"There's going to be a race here in the park next weekend," Barbie said. "And the winner gets a pair of professional in-line skates from Mr. Will's sporting goods store. Are you girls interested in entering?"

"We sure are!" Amy and Diane cheered.

Barbie smiled. "Then we better start practicing," she said.

With only a week to get ready, Barbie and the girls worked extra hard every afternoon. First they would warm up with some stretches, and then they would do laps around the park.

When Barbie said, "All right girls, that's enough for today!" Amy would always plead, "Just one more lap, Barbie!"

And Diane would say, "No! Let's make it two!"

The day before the race, the girls skated to the tree as they always did, but when they got there this time . . .

"I won!" yelled Amy.

"No, you didn't! I got here first. You saw me, Barbie—tell her I won!" replied Diane.

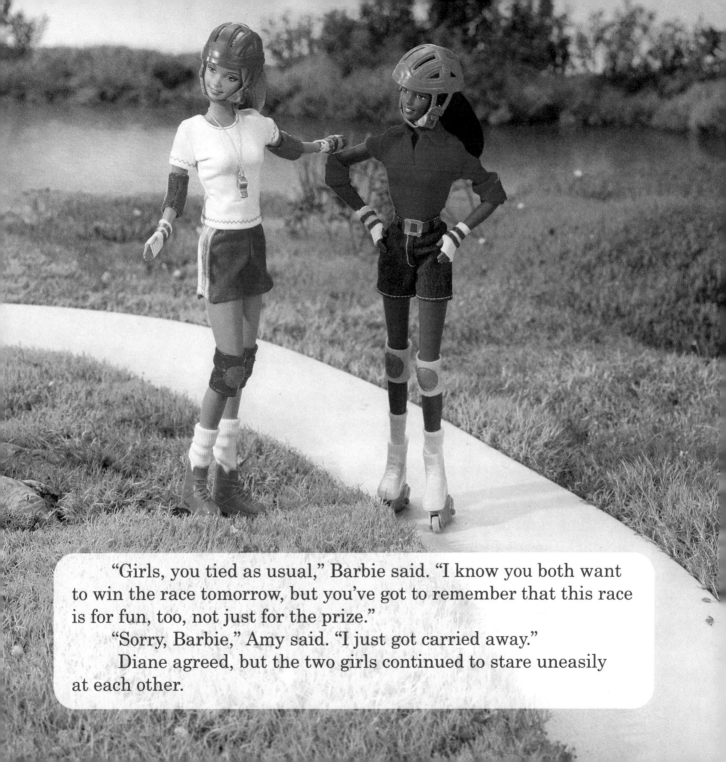

"Girls, you tied as usual," Barbie said. "I know you both want to win the race tomorrow, but you've got to remember that this race is for fun, too, not just for the prize."

"Sorry, Barbie," Amy said. "I just got carried away."

Diane agreed, but the two girls continued to stare uneasily at each other.

The next day Amy, Diane, and all the other skaters arrived in the park for the big race. Mr. Will had already put the new skates on display.

"Those skates are going to be mine when I cross the finish line," Amy said with confidence.

"The winner gets the skates," Diane replied. "And the winner's going to be me!"

"We'll see about that!" Amy said.

1st Place Prize

When it was time, the racers gathered at the starting line.
"I know you're all eager to begin," Mr. Will said. "Barbie, will you do us the honor of starting the race?"
Everyone cheered!

"On your mark," Barbie said into the megaphone. "Get set."
All the racers crouched into position. Amy and Diane darted a quick
look at each other. "GO!"
Everyone was off like a shot!

Amy and Diane quickly took the lead. They were so far out in front that one of them was sure to win.

No sooner would Amy pull ahead than Diane would catch up and pass her. They were neck and neck. They whizzed along faster than either one of them had ever skated before!

Suddenly, Amy tumbled hard to the ground. One of her skate wheels had hit a small rock and tripped her! Diane kept skating—nothing could stop her from winning now.

But, as Diane raced on, she remembered what Barbie had said about just having fun. "It's not like blading is my career," Diane mumbled to herself. Without another thought, she wheeled around and raced back to her friend.

"Are you all right?" Diane asked.

"I tripped and hurt my leg," Amy replied.

"I'll go get help," Diane said.

"But you won't win the skates," Amy said.

Diane winked at her friend. "That's OK," she said. "I've already got a pair."

Diane skated as fast as she could back down the path to Barbie. The other racers shot past her.

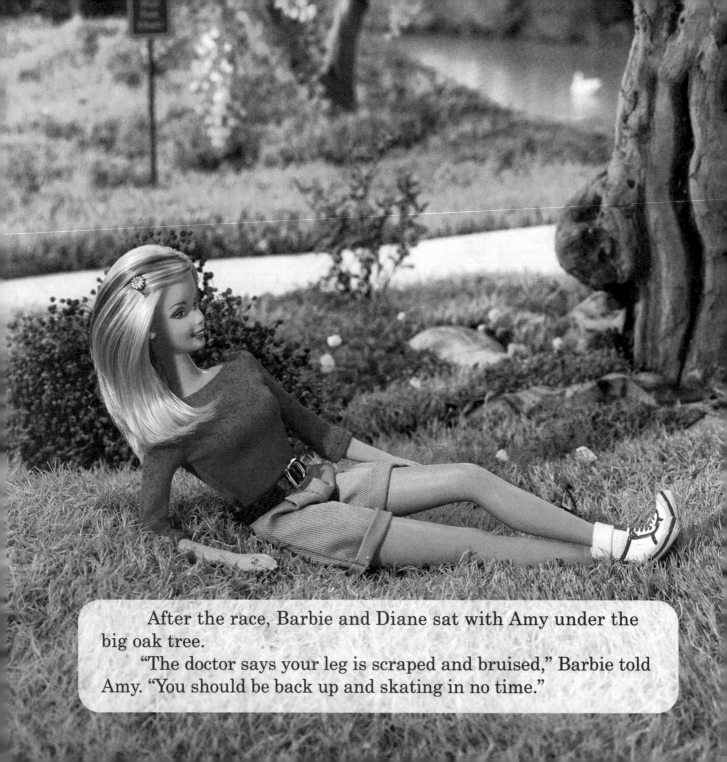

After the race, Barbie and Diane sat with Amy under the big oak tree.

"The doctor says your leg is scraped and bruised," Barbie told Amy. "You should be back up and skating in no time."

"I'm proud of you for going to get help, Diane," Barbie continued. "I know how much you both wanted to win."

"You've always taught us that having fun and doing our best is important, Barbie," Diane said, putting her arm around Amy. "I would never want to lose a friend over a pair of skates."

Just then Mr. Will walked up. He was holding something behind his back. "I'd like to present you two with these," he said.

He handed each girl a pair of skates! "You girls know what sportsmanship is all about—taking care of each other," he said. "And that's what makes you both winners."

"Thank you, Mr. Will," both girls said. They were delighted.

"Hey, Mr. Will, I have a great idea!" Amy said, slipping on just one of her new skates. "How about a three-legged race?" Amy threw her arm around Diane's shoulder.

Barbie and Mr. Will laughed.

"Barbie, with girls like these, you must be the best coach in the world," he said.